When a Line Bends . . . A Shape Begins

Rhonda Gowler Greene

Illustrated by James Kaczman

Houghton Mifflin Company
Boston

For my family — Gary, Matt, Aaron, Lianna and Brad — with love, R.G.G.

For Henry, happy first birthday, May 22 —J.K.

www.houghtonmifflinbooks.com

LIBRARY OF CONGRESS CATALOGING-IN-PUBLICATION DATA
Greene, Rhonda Gowler.
When a line bends—a shape begins
by Rhonda Gowler Greene; illustrated by James Kaczman.
p. cm.
Summary: Rhymed text describes how shapes are made from simple lines.
Some of the verses appear on the page in the shape they describe.
RNF ISBN 0-395-78606-1 PAP ISBN 0-618-15241-5
[1. Shape—Fiction. 2. Line (Art)—Fiction. 3. Visual poetry.
4. Stories in rhyme.] I. Kaczman, James, ill. II. Title.
PZ8.3.G824.Wh 1997
[E]—dc20 96-13717 CIP AC

Manufactured in China
SCP 20 19 18 17 16 15 14 13

A line is thin. A line is narrow —
curved like a worm, straight as an arrow.

A line is a jump rope, black ants in a row,
a tug-of-war game and a violin bow,
a tall pole for fishing, a leash and a trail,
a kite string, a shoelace, a whisker, a tail.

Yes, a line is fine, but when a line swerves,
when a line bends, watch what can happen . . .
a shape begins!

A square is four sides all the same —
the boxes of a hopscotch game,
a patch to cover up your knee,
a present sent from you to me,

a checkerboard of red and black,
blocks to build with, share and stack.
A cracker is a square to eat.
A square dance is for happy feet.

TAXI

A rectangle is like a square
with something rearranged.
Two sides are long
and two are short.
The four sides now
are changed.
Rectangle's a book to read,
a window and a door,
a picture hanging on the wall,
a rug that warms the floor,
a sign for selling lemonade,
a box that you can hide in,
a letter from the postman,
and a wagon two can ride in.

A
triangle
is three — three
sides, three corners
too — the white sail of a
boat, a tent built just for you.

A
jack-o'-
lantern's eyes,
a wicked witch's hat,
the beak of a black crow,
the pricked ears of a cat.

An
instru-
ment to ring,
the pyramids of
old, a lunch of jam and
bread, a napkin in a fold.

A
diamond
sits upon a point. Its
four sides are the same. A giant
green one is the infield of a baseball
game. Yellow ones along the road serve as
warning signs. Black and white ones stand out bold
in fancy floor designs. Babies' gates are wooden
ones that you can stretch or squeeze.
A ballerina's legs form one
when bending at the
knees

.

A circle's
a button, a sock hole to
mend, a shiny blue marble, a
penny to spend, a bubble, a yo-yo,
a red hula-hoop, the bowl Mom fills
with hot noodle soup, a nest in a tree,
a cookie to eat, cymbals to clang,
a big drum to beat, bicycle wheels,
a tin tambourine, a tiny,
curled kitten, a crown
for a queen.

An oval's
like a circle,
except it's not as
stout. Two sides go in
to make it thin. Two other
sides go out. Oval is a turtle's
shell, a way-up-high balloon,
a beetle and a jellybean, the
curved scoop of a spoon. It's
a mirror made to look in,
an egg all colored bright,
a mouth that's filled
with singing and a
baby bundled
tight.

Star is a five-pointed shape shining bright. Star shares the sky with the moon late at night. It tops tinseled trees in a season so merry. It sits on the tip of the wand of a fairy. Gold ones are given for good work in schools. The sheriff's star warns the bad guys of rules. A shooting star vanishes quick with a — S W I S H ! Star is even the shape of a fish.

Heart goes beat-ba-beat-ba-beat inside you all the time. It also is the shape that says, I love you, Valentine.

A crescent is a slender shape — a yellow fruit to eat, a hammock strung between two trees for Dad to rest his feet. It is a smile when curving up, when down it is a frown. It is the moon when day is done that hangs above a town

An octagon has many sides. All counted, there are eight. You see it at the corner. It tells the cars to wait.

STOP

Shapes are here. Shapes are there.
Wherever you look — a circle, a square,
a diamond, octagon, crescent, or star —
shapes to discover wherever you are!

A rectangle, triangle, oval, or heart —
shapes with a curve or a corner to start.
Anywhere, everywhere, shapes big and small —
dependable, bendable lines make them all!